Rescue Patrol

adapted by Catherine Lukas
based on the original teleplay
by McPaul Smith
illustrated by The Artifact Group

SCHOLASTIC INC.

New York Toronto London Auckland Sydney
Mexico City New Delhi Hong Kong Buenos Aires

Based on the TV series *Nick Jr. The Backyardigans*™ as seen on Nick Jr.®

No part of this publication may be reproduced,
stored in a retrieval system, or transmitted in any form
or by any means, electronic, mechanical, photocopying,
recording, or otherwise, without written permission of
the publisher. For information regarding permission, write to
Simon Spotlight, Simon & Schuster Children's Publishing Division,
1230 Avenue of the Americas, New York, NY 10020.

ISBN-13: 978-0-439-87024-5
ISBN-10: 0-439-87024-0

12 11 10 9 8 7 6 5 4 3 2 1   6 7 8 9 10 11/0

Printed in the U.S.A.
First Scholastic printing, December 2006

"We are Mounties on duty!

We have a big job," says .

TYRONE

"We guard a snow ,"

FORT

says .

PABLO

"Inside the  is a big  ,"
FORT   SNOWBALL

says  .
TYRONE

"Yes," says .
PABLO

"We must guard our
SNOWBALL

from  burglars."
SNOWBALL

"We are  patrollers!

We have a big job!"

says UNIQUA.

"Yes," says  TASHA .

"We rescue people

who are stuck

in the ❄❄ SNOW ."

"Yum! That hot  COCOA smells good," says UNIQUA.

"We save the  COCOA

for the people

we rescue!" says TASHA .

" , do you see any burglars?" asks .

PABLO

SNOWBALL

TYRONE

"Not yet," says .

PABLO

"Do you see anyone who needs help in the  ?"

SNOW

asks  .

TASHA

"Not yet," says .

UNIQUA

"Look! Someone is coming!"

says  .

TYRONE

"Help me close the 🚪 !"

DOOR

"I heard a call for help!"

says .

TASHA

"It came from that  !"

FORT

"  patrollers to the rescue!"

SKI

says .

UNIQUA

"To the roof!" says  TYRONE.

"We can see better

from up there!"

"We can climb this  ."

LADDER

The  slips on the ice .

LADDER

PABLO and **TYRONE**

land in the soft ❄❄ .
SNOW

 and

TASHA UNIQUA

pull  and

PABLO TYRONE

out of the .

SNOW

"We saved you!" says .

TASHA

"Thanks," says  .
PABLO

"We must have scared

away the ⚪ burglars,"
SNOWBALL

says 🐷 .
TYRONE

"We Mounties did our job!"

says .

TYRONE

"We  patrollers did our job!"

SKI

says ⬤.

TASHA

"Who wants a snack?"

asks  .

UNIQUA

"We have hot ☕ !"

COCOA